WALT DISNEY PRODUCTIONS

presents

Goofy
and the Magic Fish

Random House
New York

First American Edition
Copyright © 1979 by Walt Disney Productions.
All rights reserved under International and
Pan-American Copyright Conventions. Published in the
United States by Random House, Inc., New York,
and simultaneously in Canada by Random House
of Canada Limited, Toronto. Originally published in Denmark as
FEDTMULE OG DEN FANTASTISKE FISK by Gutenberghus Bladene,
Copenhagen. Copyright © 1978 by Walt Disney Productions.
ISBN: 0–394–84158–1.   ISBN: 0–394–94158–6 (lib. bdg.)
Manufactured in the United States of America.
90   A B C D E F G H I J K

There was once a fisherman named Goofy.
He lived in a little house by the sea.

Every morning he went fishing
in his little boat.
He threw his net into the water.
He pulled up a net full of fish.

Every night Goofy ate supper
and went to bed.
Nothing different ever happened.

Then one day something
VERY different happened.
A great big fish got
caught in Goofy's net!

Goofy had to pull and pull
with all his might.

At last he pulled the fish
into his boat.

Goofy was very surprised.

The fish was bigger than HE was!
Goofy was even more surprised when
the fish began to talk.

"Listen, my friend," said the fish.
"I'm magic. Magic fish taste terrible.
Put me back in the water and let me be."

Goofy was glad to get rid of
the talking fish.

He put it back into the water.

But the fish popped back up and said,
"Is there anything you want, my friend?
You have been kind to me, so I will make
one wish come true."

"Really?" said Goofy. "Then I wish
I were a farmer. That would make my life
much easier."

POOF!

Suddenly Goofy was standing in
the middle of a pretty little farm.

There were cows in the barnyard,
ducks in the pond, and geese in the lane.

There was everything a farmer needs.

"This is the life!"
thought Goofy.

But he soon realized there was also work
to be done.

He had to milk the cows...and feed the pigs.

He had to feed the chickens...

...and plow the fields.

He had to chase
the pigs out of
the vegetable garden...

...and the chickens
out of the cow shed.

He had to chase the cows
out of the cornfield...

...the rabbits out of
the carrot patch...

...and the ducks out of
the flower garden.

Before the day was over,
Goofy was very tired.
　　He was too tired to fix the fences.
He was even too tired to wonder why
the wagon was on top of the haystack.

"Farming is hard work," he thought.
Then he remembered the magic fish.

Goofy went back to his boat
and rowed out to sea.
He called to the magic fish.
"Oh, magic fish, please hear my call.
I want just one more wish, that's all."

Up popped the great big fish.
"Back so soon?" asked the fish.
"Oh, let me be a rich sea captain
instead of a farmer," said Goofy.
"Then I would not have to work so hard."

POOF!
Suddenly Goofy
was standing at the helm
of a handsome sailing ship.

"This is the life!" thought Goofy.

The ship sailed into a harbor.
The cargo was brought on shore
as Goofy played a tune.
He was very happy.

The **Golden Horse Hotel**

Then Goofy went to stay
at the finest hotel in town.

There he ate an expensive dinner
with two other rich people.
He told them many stories
about his adventures at sea.

That night robbers sneaked
into his room.

When Goofy woke up, he saw that he had
nothing left at all.

Even his pet parrot was stolen.

He was ordered out of the hotel
because he could not pay his bill.

Once again he rowed out to sea
and called to the magic fish.
"Oh, magic fish, please hear my call.
I want just one more wish, that's all."

Once again the fish popped up.
"What is it this time?" asked the fish.
"Oh, I wish I were a king instead of
a sea captain!" said Goofy. "A king
never has any problems!"

POOF!

Suddenly Goofy was sitting on a throne
inside a splendid castle.

The royal guards were guarding him.

The royal knights were bowing to him.
The royal fiddlers were fiddling
his favorite royal tune.
"This is the life!" thought Goofy.

Goofy was trying to decide what to have
for lunch when the royal messenger
rushed up.

"Your majesty!" cried the messenger.
"Your soldiers are rising up against you!"

Goofy climbed the steps
that led to the top
of the highest tower.
When he looked
out the window,
he was very surprised.

There, beyond the moat, all his soldiers
were gathered together.

"We want another king!" they cried.
"King Goofy is no good!"

"This is ridiculous," thought Goofy.
"I have done nothing at all!"

(In fact, this just might have been the problem!)

King Goofy ran out the back door
just as fast as his royal legs would go.

He ran to the seashore and found his old boat.

Goofy rowed out to sea.

Up popped the magic fish.

"Is there also something wrong with being
a king?" asked the fish.

"Indeed there is," said Goofy. "All my soldiers
are against me. They say I am a bad king.
Please let me be a fisherman again!"

POOF!

Suddenly Goofy was sitting on the
porch of his own little house.

Everything was just the same
as it had been.

"This is the life!" thought Goofy.

And Goofy never called the magic fish again.